To Ivo — *JW*

To my biggest beloved
kisser, Luca — *JA*

SIMON & SCHUSTER BOOKS FOR YOUNG READERS
An imprint of Simon & Schuster Children's Publishing Division
1230 Avenue of the Americas, New York, New York 10020
Text copyright © 2010 by Joanna Walsh
Illustrations copyright © 2010 by Giuditta Gaviraghi
Originally published in Great Britain in 2010 by Simon and Schuster UK Ltd.
Published by arrangement with Simon and Schuster UK Ltd.
First US edition 2011
All rights reserved, including the right of reproduction in whole or in part in any form.
SIMON & SCHUSTER BOOKS FOR YOUNG READERS is a trademark of Simon & Schuster, Inc.
For information about special discounts for bulk purchases, please contact Simon & Schuster
Special Sales at 1-866-506-1949 or business@simonandschuster.com.
The Simon & Schuster Speakers Bureau can bring authors to your live event. For more information or to book an event,
contact the Simon & Schuster Speakers Bureau at 1-866-248-3049 or visit our website at www.simonspeakers.com.
Manufactured in China · 1210 SUK
2 4 6 8 10 9 7 5 3
CIP data for this book is available from the Library of Congress.
ISBN 978-1-4424-2769-3
ISBN-13 978-0-8570-7399-0 (eBook)

The Biggest Kiss

Joanna Walsh

Illustrated by Judi Abbot

A Paula Wiseman Book

Simon & Schuster Books for Young Readers

New York   London   Toronto   Sydney

Kisses on noses,

kisses on toes-es.

Sudden **kisses** when you least supposes.

Who likes to **kiss**?

I do! I do! Even the shy do.

Why not try, too?

Frogs like to **kiss,**

and dogs like to **kiss.**

'normous
elephants do.

Little tiny ants do.

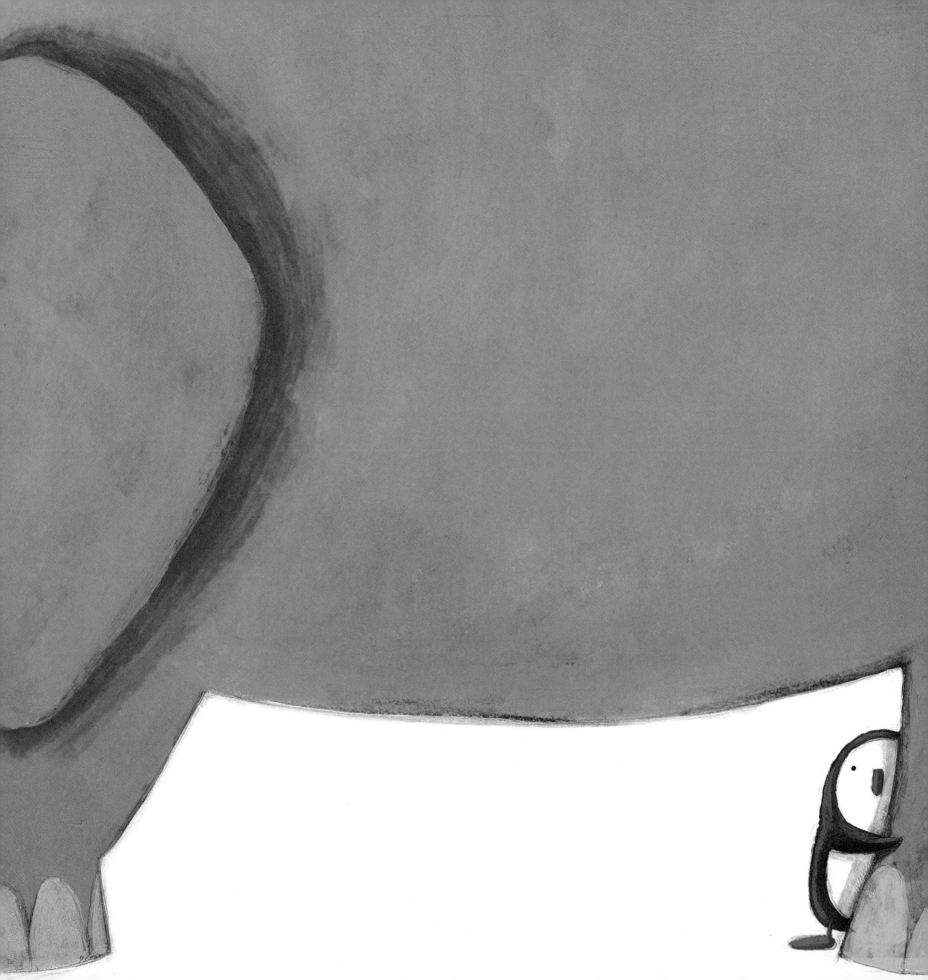

Do worms **kiss** underground, with the soil all around?

Do fish **kiss**
like this —

splosh,

splash,

splish?

Some **kisses** are misses,
they land on the ear or near.
But **kisses** with lipstick stick like . . .

a **kiss** with honey,

a **kiss** that's yummy,

a **kiss** on the elbow,

a **kiss** on the tummy.

The rain's **kiss** on your skin is fun.

The snow's **kiss** on your face is ace.

The
TALLEST
kiss is a
tricky kind.

The smallest **kiss** is hard to find.

Bye-bye
kisses,

fly-high
kisses,

eye-dry
kisses,

all my
kisses.

I wish for a **kiss** before breakfast,
to start the day right.

And a **kiss** at the end
to say, "Good night!"

I've had all these **kisses,**
and lots more too.

But the very
best kiss . . .

is a **kiss** from you!